That Baby in the Manger

ANNE E. NEUBERGEF
Illustrated by Chloe E. Pitkoff

PARACLETE PRESS
BREWSTER, MASSACHUSETTS

The church was quiet until a door opened and several children trooped in, their heavy boots breaking the silence. A young teacher followed them.

"Oh look! It's all set up!" one little voice exclaimed.

In the last pew, Mr. Gonzales looked up from his prayer. Every morning he stopped in on his way home after his night shift of work. Usually it was quiet in the church but today he watched as the first graders of the parish school came in, heading straight for the large crèche.

3

"There's Mary!" a girl shouted.

"I like that shepherd with a lamb on his shoulders," another child added.

"How many sheep are there?" the teacher asked.

As some children counted out loud, one little boy asked, "Where's Baby Jesus?"

He sounded disappointed.

Before the teacher could answer, a side door opened and Fr. Prak came in. "Good morning!" he called cheerfully. "Isn't our crèche beautiful?"

Several children nodded, but the boy asked again, "Fr. Prak, where's Baby Jesus?"

Mr. Gonzales could see the child now. He wore a blue stocking cap and his face was serious and intent, almost worried.

"The time to put the Jesus statue in hasn't come yet," Father Prak said. "This is Advent, the waiting time. We're waiting for Jesus's birthday, which is Christmas morning. Then we'll place him in the manger."

"I remember that statue," a girl said. "He has blonde curls."

Mr. Gonzales noticed that this little girl had straight hair as dark as the night sky.

Father Prak looked surprised, but the teacher just smiled.

The priest ran his hand through his own black curls. "Yes, I think you're right," he answered the girl. "You have a good memory."

A freckle-faced boy pointed and said. "So does the Mary statue. My mom says that Mary probably had dark hair."

Father Prak said, "Remember, these are just statues. An artist made them. We set up the stable and statues every year to help us think about Jesus's birth in a stable."

The boy wrinkled his freckled nose and peered at the statues more closely. "So what color eyes did Jesus have?" he asked.

"Jesus was born in a part of the world where most people had very dark hair, so he and Mary probably had very dark hair. And dark eyes too," Father Prak answered, then glanced at his watch. "Now let's get started on practicing for the children's Mass on Christmas morning."

The teacher began, "You will each be sitting with your families at first, then come up to sing. . . ."

Mr. Gonzales finished his prayers and then quietly left the church. He was tired, as he always was after working all night, but he wasn't sure he could sleep now.

As he walked the cold streets to his home, he kept hearing the little girl's words, "He has blonde curls."

Mr. Gonzales knew there was nothing wrong with blonde curls, but he kept thinking of his own little girl, now all grown up. Long ago, she had looked at that same crèche in that same church and said, "Papa, Baby Jesus doesn't look like me at all!"

That Christmas, she had gotten a baby doll with dark eyes and hair. For weeks, she pretended that her doll was Baby Jesus.

He smiled as he remembered, but he couldn't forget the faces of the children he had seen today.

At home, he rummaged around in some boxes stored in a closet. When he found what he was looking for, he smiled, and then went off to bed.

A few days before Christmas, Mr. Gonzales again pulled the box from the closet. He took out his daughter's old doll, the one she had pretended was Baby Jesus. He dusted the doll clean.

Then he took an old bed sheet and cut it into long strips. These he wound around the doll, so it would be wrapped in swaddling clothes.

With the doll in his arms, Mr. Gonzales left his house, heading for the church. He slipped into the side door. Earlier, people had been busy decorating with poinsettias and evergreens, but now no one was there but him.

He walked up to the crèche. The Mary and Joseph statues still waited, looking at the empty manger. Mr. Gonzales knelt down. He adjusted the swaddling clothes on the doll and gently placed it into the manger. Then he laid a piece of paper in the straw next to the doll. He said a prayer before leaving.

The next morning, Fr. Prak came in, stomping snow off his boots. Then he noticed the doll in the manger. Puzzled, he went closer.

Picking up the paper, he read, "Dear Father Prak, I heard the children asking you about Baby Jesus's hair and eye color. I remember my own daughter asking me the same thing. I thought her old doll, which she pretended was Baby Jesus, might be a more accurate image of Jesus for the children. Sincerely, Antonio Gonzales."

Fr. Prak smiled, thinking of the many things Mr. Gonzales had done for this church. Looking at the doll, he chuckled at the swaddling clothes.

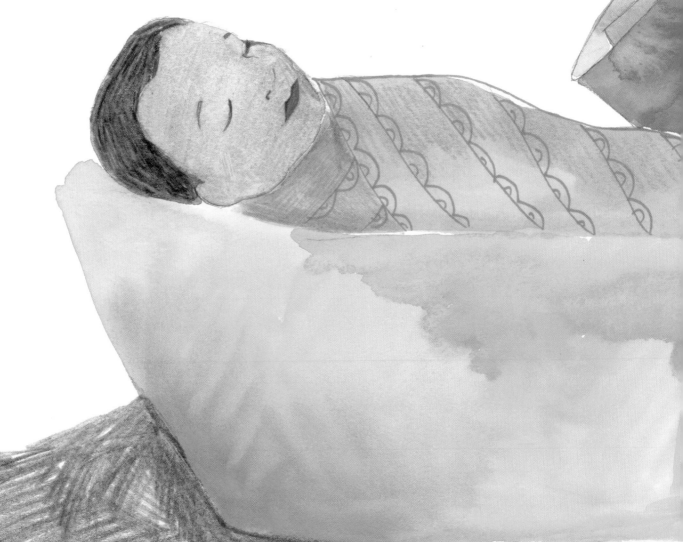

Mr. Gonzales was right, of course. It was important that people understood that a baby born in Bethlehem probably did not look like the statue they had. This doll would be Baby Jesus this year.

But there was something more important. Children should know that no matter what color Jesus's hair was, he came for all of them, no matter what they looked like themselves. Jesus loves them all.

But how could they come to learn this? Fr. Prak sat down near the crèche and began to pray. When he finished, he went over to talk with the first graders.

Christmas morning dawned and soon the church was full of warmth and excitement, and of smiling adults and wiggling children. Soft candlelight shown on the figures in the crèche.

Mr. Gonzales sat down with his family near the front of the church. "Look at the manger," he whispered to his daughter. "Does that Baby Jesus look familiar?"

Everyone stood as Mass started. The first graders filed up to the crèche to lead the congregation in song. Father Prak tried to keep a straight face.

Every child was carrying a doll!

There were dolls
with long, silky
hair, some tied into
pony tails with
bright ribbons.
Some children held
soft dolls with hair
of yarn and shiny
button eyes. One doll
smiled bravely, even
though she had one
eye missing.

Some dolls had
painted-on hair, and
a few sported spiky
hair that had been cut
off by small children
with blunt scissors.

There were dolls with black hair, dolls with red hair, some with blonde and others with brown. And, one doll had blue hair.

The children held their dolls as lovingly as Mary held Jesus so long ago.

"Away in the manger, no crib for a bed, the little Lord Jesus lay down his sweet head. . . ." The children sang and everyone else joined in.

When the song was finished, each child stepped up to the stable and gently placed his or her doll close to the manger before going to sit down.

Mr. Gonzales put his arm around his daughter. They were both smiling.

Father Prak gave a deep, contented sigh. He had received a great Christmas gift: an answer to his prayer.

TO OUR EZRA, LITTLE PROPHET
—YOU ARE LOVED—

2017 First Printing
That Baby in the Manger

Text copyright © 2017 by Anne E. Neuberger
Illustrations copyright © 2017 by Chloe E. Pitkoff

ISBN 978-1-61261-946-0

The Paraclete Press name and logo (dove on cross) are trademarks of Paraclete Press, Inc.

Library of Congress Cataloging-in-Publication Data

Names: Neuberger, Anne E., 1953- author. | Pitkoff, Chloe E., illustrator.
Title: That baby in the manger / Anne E. Neuberger ; illustrated by Chloe E. Pitkoff.
Description: Brewster, Massachusetts : Paraclete Press, [2017] | Summary: "As
the children of a small church struggle with the portrayal of the Holy
Family in the Nativity scene as European—not Middle Eastern and not
necessarily like them—they learn more about Jesus's love for all
children"— Provided by publisher.
Identifiers: LCCN 2017018857 | ISBN 9781612619460 (hardcover dust-jacket)
Subjects: LCSH: Jesus Christ—Nativity—Juvenile fiction. | CYAC: Jesus
Christ—Nativity—Fiction. | Christmas—Fiction.
Classification: LCC PZ7.N4395 Th 2017 | DDC [E]—dc23
LC record available at https://lccn.loc.gov/2017018857

10 9 8 7 6 5 4 3 2 1

Published by Paraclete Press
Brewster, Massachusetts
www.paracletepress.com

Printed in the United States of America